W9-DET-026

INSIDE MAJOR LEAGUE BASEBALL™

BASEBALL IN THE AMERICAN LEAGUE CENTRAL DIVISION

CHICAGO

WHITE SOX

CLEVELAND

INDIANS

DETROIT

TIGERS

KANSAS CITY

ROYALS

MINNESOTA

TWINS

rosen publishing's
rosen
central®

New York

JASON PORTERFIELD

Published in 2009 by The Rosen Publishing Group, Inc.
29 East 21st Street, New York, NY 10010

Library of Congress Cataloging-in-Publication Data

Porterfield, Jason.
Baseball in the American League Central Division / Jason Porterfield.—1st ed.
     p. cm.
Includes bibliographical references and index.
ISBN-13: 978-1-4358-5042-2 (library binding)
ISBN-13: 978-1-4358-5416-1 (pbk)
ISBN-13: 978-1-4358-5422-2 (6 pack)
1. American League of Professional Baseball Clubs—History. I. Title.
GV875.A15P67 2009
796.357'640973—dc22

                                                                    2008022085

Manufactured in the United States of America

On the cover: On baseball cards, top to bottom: Jim Thome of the Chicago White Sox; Victor Martinez of the Cleveland Indians; Magglio Ordoñez of the Detroit Tigers; Gil Meche of the Kansas City Royals; Justin Morneau of the Minnesota Twins. Foreground: Joe Mauer of the Minnesota Twins. Background: Cleveland's Progressive Field, shown in 2005, when it was named Jacobs Field.

CONTENTS

NOV 7 - 2008

INTRODUCTION

The 101st World Series, played in 2005, featured two teams long overdue for a World Series title. The Houston Astros made their very first World Series appearance in 44 years. The Chicago White Sox had not been to the World Series since 1959, and they hadn't won a title since 1917. Every game in the series was decided by two or fewer runs, with Chicago winning the first three through a mix of superior starting pitching and timely hits. The fourth game of the series turned into a pitcher's duel between Freddy Garcia of the White Sox and Brandon Backe of the Astros. The game remained scoreless until White Sox outfielder Jermaine Dye finally singled home a run in the seventh inning to break the tie. The Astros threatened to score in the eighth, but the White Sox defense held onto the lead. The White Sox won the game 1–0, giving the team its first World Series title in decades and giving the American League Central division its first World Series title ever.

In addition to the White Sox, the teams making up the American League Central have been some of the most successful in Major League

MARK BUEHRLE
#56

Exelon.

Baseball. All five teams—the Chicago White Sox, the Cleveland Indians, the Detroit Tigers, the Kansas City Royals, and the Minnesota Twins—have won at least one World Series title in their histories. They have been successful in recent history, as well. AL Central teams have made four World Series appearances since the league formed in 1994, and the division has produced two American League MVPs (Most Valuable Players) and three Cy Young Award winners.

Early on, the slugging and slick-fielding Cleveland Indians dominated the division,

U.S. Cellular Field in Chicago *(background)*, during the 2005 American League Championship Series. Chicago White Sox slugger Jermaine Dye *(above)* was named World Series MVP in 2005.

while the other teams seemed to be in a constant state of rebuilding. When the Indians themselves had to rebuild with younger players, other teams filled the gap with different approaches. The Twins won four division titles by excelling at fundamental baseball, with good pitching, steady hitting, and solid fielding and base running. The White Sox, Tigers, and Indians have all had recent success by building solid teams around good pitching.

CHAPTER ONE

BASEBALL IN THE AL CENTRAL

The American League began as an organization of minor league teams then called the Western League. Throughout the 1890s, the National League was baseball's only major league, but Western League president Bancroft Johnson decided that his teams could compete with the National League. In 1899, the six-team Western League added

Cleveland Indians right-hander Bob Feller *(above, left)* was one of his era's most dominant pitchers, despite missing four seasons (1942–1945) to fight in World War II.

teams in Chicago and Washington, D.C., and changed its name to the American League.

In 1901, the American League officially became a major league. Of the eight charter member teams, four eventually landed in the American League Central: the Chicago White Stockings (White Sox), the Cleveland Blues (Indians), the Detroit Tigers, and the Washington Senators.

As time passed, baseball evolved and the league grew. Home runs became common with the emergence of sluggers like Babe Ruth in

Jackie Robinson became the first African American to play for a major league team when he joined the Brooklyn Dodgers in 1947. Here, the speedy Robinson is shown stealing home in a game against the Chicago Cubs in 1949.

the 1920s. Pitching also changed, with 30-game winners becoming increasingly rare. African Americans, once excluded from playing in the major leagues, were recruited to play after Jackie Robinson broke baseball's color barrier in 1947.

Teams also changed, sometimes relocating to other cities. In 1961, for example, the American League's Washington Senators relocated to Minneapolis and became the Minnesota Twins. Other teams, including the Kansas City Royals, joined the American League, and by 1969, there were 12 AL teams.

The 1969 season saw both the American League and the National League split into East and West divisions. The play-off structure also changed that year, as the team with the best record in each division played each other in a best-of-five-games American League Championship Series (ALCS). The winner would go on to play in the World Series against the team that won the National League Championship Series (NLCS).

The Pilots moved to Milwaukee to become the Milwaukee Brewers in 1970. Two more teams—the Seattle Mariners and the Toronto Blue Jays—were added in 1974, giving the American League 14 teams. The American League added one more team, the Tampa Bay Devil Rays, in 1998. At the same time, the Milwaukee Brewers joined the National League, giving both leagues 14 teams.

The 1994 Realignment

While the number of teams in the American League has remained constant since 1974, the structure of the league changed once again in 1994. Teams from the East and West divisions of both the American League and the National League were split off to form new Central

Teams tend to play a little harder against their Central division rivals. Here, White Sox shortstop Juan Uribe breaks up a potential double play against the Minnesota Twins during a game in 2008.

divisions. Teams in the new American League Central included the Chicago White Sox, Minnesota Twins, and Kansas City Royals of the old American League West, along with the Milwaukee Brewers and Cleveland Indians of the old American League East. The Detroit Tigers joined the division from the AL East in 1998, when the Brewers jumped to the National League Central.

The realignment made sense for many reasons. All five teams are located in the American Midwest, three of them bordering the Great Lakes. They have far more in common with each other than with teams located on either the East or the West Coast. At one point, their home cities all had economies that were dependent upon manufacturing or agriculture. The teams and their fans all endure the same hot Midwestern summers and brutally cold winters. It also became easier to build fan interest by developing rivalries with nearby cities, giving the AL Central teams an economic boost by guaranteeing large crowds at some games.

Along with the team structure of each league, the play-offs also changed in 1994. Instead of having just two division champions per league, there were now three. A new round of play-off games was introduced. Two division champions would play each other in a best-of-five League Division Series (LDS), while the third division winner

AL Central Champs
(since 1994 realignment)

1994	Chicago White Sox*
1995	Cleveland Indians
1996	Cleveland Indians
1997	Cleveland Indians
1998	Cleveland Indians
1999	Cleveland Indians
2000	Chicago White Sox
2001	Cleveland Indians
2002	Minnesota Twins
2003	Minnesota Twins
2004	Minnesota Twins
2005	Chicago White Sox
2006	Minnesota Twins
2007	Cleveland Indians

* (Strike-shortened season; no play-offs)

American League Central Team History
(since realignment in 1994)

	YEAR ENTERED THE AL CENTRAL	AL CENTRAL CHAMPIONSHIPS	AMERICAN LEAGUE PENNANTS	WORLD SERIES CHAMPIONSHIPS
Chicago White Sox	1994	3*	1	1
Cleveland Indians	1994	7	2	0
Detroit Tigers	1998	0	1	0
Kansas City Royals	1994	0	0	0
Minnesota Twins	1994	4	0	0

* Includes 1994; Chicago was in first place in the division when the players' strike ended the season.

would play a wild card team, the division runner-up with the best record. The winners of these series would go on to face each other in the League Championship Series (LCS).

Today's American League Central

The team lineup of the American League Central hasn't changed since Detroit joined in 1998. Today, the division is made up of five teams:

St. Louis Cardinals outfielder Jim Edmonds doubles off of Detroit Tigers pitcher Nate Robertson in game 3 of the 2006 World Series. The Tigers lost the series in five games.

the Chicago White Sox, the Cleveland Indians, the Detroit Tigers, the Kansas City Royals, and the Minnesota Twins. Three of these teams— the Indians, the White Sox, and the Twins—have won the AL Central division at least once. The Tigers made the play-offs, too, as the 2006 wild card team. Only the Royals have failed to make it to the play-offs since the division formed. The Indians, White Sox, and Tigers have all made it to the World Series since 1994, with the White Sox winning the title in 2005.

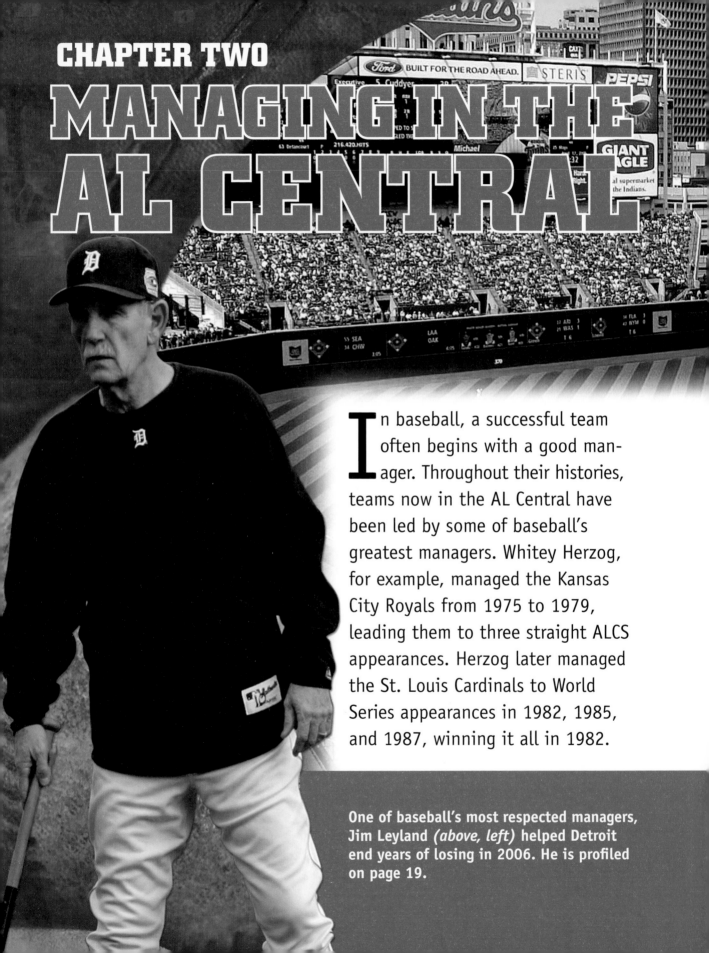

CHAPTER TWO
MANAGING IN THE AL CENTRAL

In baseball, a successful team often begins with a good manager. Throughout their histories, teams now in the AL Central have been led by some of baseball's greatest managers. Whitey Herzog, for example, managed the Kansas City Royals from 1975 to 1979, leading them to three straight ALCS appearances. Herzog later managed the St. Louis Cardinals to World Series appearances in 1982, 1985, and 1987, winning it all in 1982.

One of baseball's most respected managers, Jim Leyland *(above, left)* helped Detroit end years of losing in 2006. He is profiled on page 19.

Sparky Anderson managed the Detroit Tigers from 1979 to 1995. Prior to managing the Tigers, Anderson enjoyed great success coaching the Cincinnati Reds of the National League. Under Anderson's direction, the Reds won back-to-back World Series championships in 1975 and 1976. The Tigers won the 1984 World Series, making Anderson the first manager ever to win a World Series in each league. He retired in 1995 and was elected to the Baseball Hall of Fame in 2000.

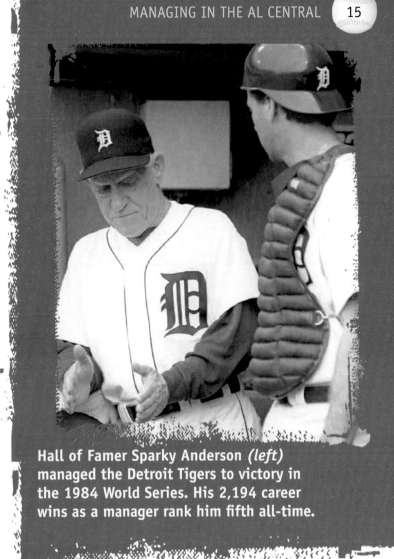

Hall of Famer Sparky Anderson *(left)* managed the Detroit Tigers to victory in the 1984 World Series. His 2,194 career wins as a manager rank him fifth all-time.

Tony La Russa managed the White Sox from 1979 to 1986, leading the team to the ALCS in 1983 and compiling a 522–210 record in Chicago. He later went on to win the 1989 World Series as manager of the Oakland Athletics. La Russa also managed the St. Louis Cardinals to victory in the 2006 World Series.

Tom Kelly won the 1987 and 1991 World Series championships while managing the Minnesota Twins. The 1991 Twins were the first team to ever win the World Series after finishing last in their division the previous year.

Since realignment in 1994, several managers have excelled at getting the best out of their teams, carrying on the great tradition established by such managers as Herzog, Anderson, La Russa, and Kelly.

Mike Hargrove—Cleveland Indians

Mike Hargrove was an All-Star first baseman before becoming manager of the Cleveland Indians in 1991. He took over a team that had not made a play-off appearance since 1954. In 1994, the first year of the AL Central, Hargrove managed his young Indians team to a winning record. They were only one game behind the White Sox in the division when a players' strike ended the season early.

The year 1994 was only the beginning. From 1995 to 1999, the Indians won the AL Central five consecutive times. They won one hundred games in 1995, the most in the major leagues that season. They went to the World Series twice, losing to the Atlanta Braves in 1995 and the Florida Marlins in 1997. Hargrove left the Indians in 1999, after they lost to Boston in the American League Division Series (ALDS). Though he went on to manage the Baltimore Orioles and the Seattle Mariners, he did not have the same success with those teams.

Ozzie Guillen—Chicago White Sox

Ozzie Guillen began his career in the major leagues as a shortstop for the White Sox. After retiring from playing, he became a coach for the Montreal Expos (now the Washington Nationals) and later for the Florida Marlins team that won the 2003 World Series. He became manager of the White Sox in 2004, leading the team to a second place finish in the division that year.

In 2005, Guillen's emphasis on solid fielding and base running—called "Ozzieball" by the Chicago media—helped the team win the AL Central. They went on to win the World Series for the first time since 1917 by sweeping the Houston Astros. Guillen was named American League Manager of the Year for the 2005 season. His outspoken personality has led to several controversies, but Guillen remains a favorite of Sox fans. He led the team to a 648–344 record through his first four seasons as manager.

Chicago White Sox manager Ozzie Guillen celebrates his team's victory in the 2005 World Series. Under Guillen, the White Sox cruised through the postseason, winning 11 games against only one loss.

Eric Wedge—Cleveland Indians

Eric Wedge became the Indians' manager in 2003, after he spent several years as a manager in the organization's minor league system. Only 35 years old, he was the youngest manager in the major leagues. In his first season, the Indians went 68–94, finishing in fourth place. The next season, they improved to 80–82. In 2005, they won 93 games and just barely missed the play-offs after being eliminated by the

White Sox on the final day of the season. Wedge finished second to Ozzie Guillen in Manager of the Year voting that season. Many expected the Indians to continue improving in 2006, but they finished a disappointing 78–84.

In 2007, Wedge's Indians bounced back to win the AL Central with a 96–66 record, taking the division title for the first time since 2001. The Indians beat the New York Yankees to win their ALDS, but they lost to the Boston Red Sox in an exciting seven-game American League Championship Series. Wedge was named 2007 American League Manager of the Year for his team's accomplishments.

Player-Managers

Once, it was common for major league teams to be managed by an active player. These player-managers not only had to make decisions about pitching rotations and batting lineups, but they also had to play their own positions in the field. Two of the more famous player-managers in history played for the Cleveland Indians. Tris Speaker was a star outfielder for the Indians from 1916 to 1926. In 1919, he became player-manager. The following year, he led the team to its first World Series title, batting .388 in the process. Speaker was elected to the Baseball Hall of Fame in 1937.

All-Star shortstop Lou Boudreau played for the Indians from 1938 to 1952. In 1942, at just 25 years old, Boudreau became the Indians' player-manager. In 1948, he had his best season, hitting .355 and leading his team to a first place tie with the Boston Red Sox. He then hit two home runs in a special one-game play-off against the Red Sox to secure the American League pennant. The Indians went on to win the World Series title in 1948. (They have not won the title since.) For his heroic efforts, Boudreau was named 1948 American League Most Valuable Player. He was elected to the Baseball Hall of Fame in 1970.

Jim Leyland—Detroit Tigers

Jim Leyland became a major league manager in 1985 with the Pittsburgh Pirates. He led that team to three consecutive National League Championship Series appearances, in 1990, 1991, and 1992. He left the Pirates in 1996 and became the manager of the Florida Marlins. The following year, Leyland led the Marlins to a World Series victory over the Cleveland Indians. He left the Marlins organization after the 1999 season.

Leyland then spent several seasons as a scout for the St. Louis Cardinals. However, when the 2005 season ended, he was hired as the manager for the Detroit Tigers. At that time, Detroit had suffered 12 straight years without a winning record, including an American League record of 119 losses, in 2003. Leyland quickly turned the Tigers around, leading them to a 95–67 record and a play-off spot as the American League wild card team. The Tigers defeated the New York Yankees and the Oakland Athletics to advance to the World Series, making Leyland just the third manager to win pennants in both the American League and the National League. The Tigers ultimately lost the World Series to the St. Louis Cardinals, but Leyland was named the 2006 American League Manager of the Year. It was the third time in his career that he was so honored, having earned the award with the Pittsburgh Pirates in 1990 and 1992.

Ron Gardenhire—Minnesota Twins

Ron Gardenhire became manager of the Minnesota Twins in 2002, following the retirement of longtime manager Tom Kelly. Gardenhire is a former major league utility infielder and minor league manager.

Minnesota Twins manager Ron Gardenhire argues with an umpire during a 2003 game against the Milwaukee Brewers. Gardenhire's fiery demeanor has won him the loyalty of his players.

Under his direction, the Twins won the AL Central in 2002, 2003, 2004, and 2006. In 2002, they advanced as far as the ALCS, losing in five games to the Anaheim Angels. Gardenhire is excitable and combative compared to his laid-back predecessor, Kelly. He inspires confidence in his players and is skilled at helping talented young players develop. Though the Twins typically have one of the smallest payrolls in Major League Baseball, Gardenhire didn't experience his first losing season until the Twins went 79–83 in 2007. As of 2007, Gardenhire had a 971–534 record as a manager.

CHAPTER THREE

WINNING IN THE AL CENTRAL

Since the AL Central formed, the race for the division championship has often been one of the most exciting in baseball. Rivalries spring up naturally among the division's teams, while others carry over to teams from other divisions or even from the National League. The Tigers and Indians are longtime rivals, going back to

Catcher A. J. Pierzynski and pitcher Bobby Jenks *(left)* of the 2005 Chicago White Sox celebrate after clinching the franchise's first World Series title since 1917.

when the two teams were both in the American League East. Detroit and Cleveland are only about four hours apart by car, making it easy for each team's fans to travel to the other team's park. The rivalry developed during the 1920s, 1930s, and 1940s, as both teams enjoyed success, including winning world championships. The rivalry has intensified in recent years, with both the Tigers and Indians becoming competitive once again in the AL Central.

The White Sox and Twins have played in the same division since 1969, when the old American League West formed. However, a real rivalry between the two teams has developed only in recent years. In 2000, the White Sox won their first AL Central title. The Twins then won the title for three straight years in 2002, 2003, and 2004. The White Sox broke the streak in 2005 and went on to win the World Series. Despite keeping most of their team intact, Chicago lost the division in 2006 to the Twins.

Royals–Yankees Rivalry

During the late 1970s, the Kansas City Royals dominated the AL West division, while the New York Yankees dominated the AL East division. Intense postseason competition between the two teams created a strong rivalry. It wasn't unusual for pitchers on both teams to hit opposing batters, and bench-clearing brawls often interrupted games. Between 1976 and 1978, New York got the better of the rivalry, beating Kansas City in three straight AL Championship series. However, the Royals finally beat the Yankees in the play-offs in 1980 and celebrated as if they had won the World Series. Although the Royals did not make the postseason in the first 13 years after joining the division, the intense rivalry between the teams continues to this day.

White Sox–Cubs Rivalry

The Chicago White Sox and Chicago Cubs aren't even in the same league, but their rivalry is still among the most intense in baseball. Part of this has to do with geography. The Cubs play on Chicago's North Side in a traditionally residential area; the Sox play on the grittier South Side, where many of the city's factories and stockyards were once located. Both teams endured decades without a World Series win

Interleague games are a huge hit in Chicago. Here, White Sox catcher A. J. Pierzynski tags out the Cubs' Juan Pierre in a 2006 game at Wrigley Field.

until the White Sox won the championship in 2005. Every season since 1997, the two teams have played two three-game series against each other at each team's stadium, giving fans of each team an opportunity to root against their crosstown rivals.

The Division Race

Since realignment in 1994, baseball play-offs have used a two-round play-off system. In the American League, the winner of each of the three divisions makes it to the American League Division Series (ALDS). The fourth team to make the play-offs is called the wild card team. This is the second-place team with the best record. The winners of the ALDS play each other in the American League Championship Series (ALCS), a best-of-seven series, with the winner going on to play in the World Series. This system has helped to keep more teams alive in the "pennant races" that play out toward the end of the season.

Indians Dominate the New Central Division

For the first five seasons of the AL Central division, the Cleveland Indians were the most dominant team. The Indians won the division title five years in a row, from 1995 to 1999. The 1995 team had a balanced mix of experienced veterans and younger players, including Kenny Lofton, Jim Thome, and Manny Ramirez. They won 100 games during the regular season but lost in the World Series to the Atlanta Braves.

The Indians dominated the division with a good balance of offense and defense. They held on to many of their talented young sluggers and consistently had one of the best defensive teams in the majors. Their defense was led by Lofton and shortstop Omar Vizquel, both All-Stars and Gold Glove Award winners. After 1999, their defense also featured the best fielding second baseman in the game, Roberto Alomar. Cleveland made it to the World Series again in 1997, only to be beaten in seven games by the Florida Marlins.

World Champions: The 2005 White Sox

The White Sox returned to the top of the division in 2005. The team's stellar pitching staff included young guns Mark Buehrle and Jon Garland, along with veterans Freddy Garcia and José Contreras. The White Sox also had a strong offense, with team captain Paul Konerko leading the way with 40 home runs and 100 RBI. The team also got solid contributions from outfielders Jermaine Dye, Aaron Rowand, and Scott Podsednik—who stole 59 bases that season.

Though they had a 15-game lead at the beginning of August, the Sox slumped badly, allowing a young Cleveland Indians team to get within one-and-a-half games before clinching the division on September 29. The Sox then went on to win 11 of 12 postseason games, including a four-game sweep of the National League Champion Houston Astros in the World Series.

First baseman Paul Konerko helped the White Sox make it to the 2005 World Series with his bat and solid defensive play.

Parity in the AL Central

Competition in the AL Central division became more evenly balanced after the Indians' run in the late 1990s. In 2000, the White Sox emerged as the division champions behind the hitting of veteran slugger Frank Thomas and young players Paul Konerko, Carlos Lee, and Magglio Ordonez. The Sox survived a late-season run by the Indians to make their first play-off appearance since 1993, but they were swept in the first round of the play-offs by the Seattle Mariners.

From 2002 to 2004, the Minnesota Twins finished the season on top in the AL Central. None of their squads advanced in the postseason, however.

In 2006, the White Sox fell to third place in the division, behind the Twins and the Tigers. The Tigers came out of nowhere to take an early-season lead behind young pitchers Jeremy Bonderman and rookie Justin Verlander. After years of criticism for signing veteran players to bad contracts, the Tigers got excellent contributions from former All-Stars Ivan Rodriguez, Magglio Ordonez, and veteran pitchers Kenny Rogers and Todd Jones.

The Tigers led the division for much of the season, but the Minnesota Twins caught up to them behind strong pitching from starters Johan Santana and Francisco Liriano, as well as closer Joe Nathan. Twins bats played a big part, too. The young lineup included seven-time Gold Glove–winning outfielder Torii Hunter, catcher Joe Mauer, and 2006 AL MVP Justin Morneau. The Twins clinched the division on the last day of play, but the Tigers won the AL wild card and went on to their first World Series appearance since 1984. Unfortunately for Detroit fans, the Tigers lost in five games to the St. Louis Cardinals.

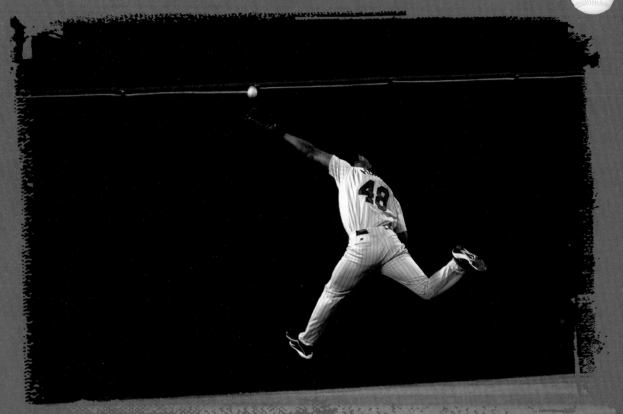

Minnesota's Torii Hunter attempts a spectacular catch during a game against the Anaheim Angels in the 2002 American League Championship Series. Hunter patrolled center field for the Twins from 1999 to 2007.

In 2007, the Tigers and the Indians battled for the division lead early in the season, but Cleveland pulled ahead. Indians pitcher C. C. Sabathia won the American League Cy Young award that season, while the team got consistent hitting from a lineup packed with young stars. Standouts included speedy center fielder Grady Sizemore and hard-hitting catcher Victor Martinez. The Indians beat the Yankees in the division series and came within one game of their first World Series appearance since 1997. However, the Boston Red Sox came back to win the ALCS in seven games.

CHAPTER FOUR
PLAYERS OF THE AL CENTRAL

Teams now in the American League Central have always had their share of great hitters and fielders, from Ty Cobb and "Shoeless" Joe Jackson in the 1910s and 1920s to current stars Curtis Granderson of the Tigers and the Twins' Joe Mauer. Hall of Fame pitchers such as the Indians' Bob Feller once dominated the American League, a role recently filled by latter-day aces like the Indians' Cliff Lee and the Tigers' Justin Verlander.

Left: Pitcher Justin Verlander quickly became the ace of Detroit's starting rotation. He was named to his first All-Star team in 2007, in only his second season.

All-Time Greats

Ty Cobb played for the Detroit Tigers from 1905 to 1926. During his long career, Cobb won a record 11 batting titles and set career records that stood for decades, including most hits, stolen bases, and runs scored. His .366 career batting average is still a record. Cobb was elected to the Hall of Fame in 1936.

Bob Feller pitched for the Cleveland Indians from 1936 to 1956, compiling a record of 266 wins against 162 losses. He remains the most dominant pitcher in Indians history and is Cleveland's career leader in wins, strikeouts, games started, and complete games. Feller also leads the Indians in no-hitters, having thrown three during his career. He was elected to the Hall of Fame in 1962.

Rod Carew played for the Twins from 1967 to 1978, winning seven batting titles during that stretch. One of the best hitters ever, he batted over .300 in 15 straight seasons. His league-leading .388 batting average in 1977 helped him capture the American League MVP that year. Carew finished his career with 3,053 hits and a .328 batting average. He was elected to the Hall of Fame in 1991.

Frank Thomas—Chicago White Sox

Many consider Frank "Big Hurt" Thomas one of the greatest hitters ever to play for the White Sox. Thomas made his major league debut with the Sox in 1990 and quickly established himself as one of the most danger-ous hitters in the game, with the ability to hit for power and a high average. He won back-to-back MVP awards, in 1993 and 1994. The big first baseman hit 40 or more homers for the team in six seasons, and he won the 1997 American League batting title with a .347 average.

In his days with the White Sox, Frank Thomas struck fear in the hearts of opposing pitchers with his huge size and physical strength.

Thomas left the White Sox after the 2005 World Series but continued playing. He hit his 500th career home run in 2007 while playing for the Toronto Blue Jays.

Johan Santana— Minnesota Twins

Since his first season as a starting pitcher with the Twins in 2003, Johan Santana has become one of the best pitchers in the major leagues. He won 15 or more games each season from 2004 to 2007. While with the Twins, Santana won the American League Cy Young award twice, in 2004 and 2006, leading the league in earned run average (ERA) both seasons. He also led the American League in strikeouts in 2004, 2005, and 2006. After the 2007 season, the Twins traded Santana to the New York Mets of the National League.

Jim Thome—Cleveland Indians, Chicago White Sox

Jim Thome helped the Indians dominate the American League Central through the division's first seasons. A prolific home run hitter, he hit

30 or more homers in seven straight seasons with the Indians, from 1996 to 2002, including a career-high 52 in 2002. He left Cleveland after that season to play for the Philadelphia Phillies for three seasons before returning to the AL Central with Chicago in 2006. Thome hit his 500th home run in 2007 as a member of the White Sox.

Jim Thome's power hitting and off-field charity work have made him a fan favorite from Philadelphia to Chicago. Thome is a five-time All-Star, for three different teams.

Justin Verlander and Curtis Granderson—Detroit Tigers

Starting pitcher Justin Verlander of the Detroit Tigers went 17–9 in 2006, his rookie year. Verlander was named the AL Rookie of the Year that season. He improved to 18–6 in 2007, throwing the first no-hitter for the Tigers since Jack Morris no-hit the Chicago White Sox in 1984.

Verlander's teammate, Curtis Granderson, had a breakout season in 2007, when he became just the third player in major league history to hit 20 home runs, 20 doubles, 20 triples, and steal 20 bases in the same season.

Curtis Granderson plays with speed and power for the Detroit Tigers. He hit 23 triples in 2007, the most in the major leagues since 1949.

C. C. Sabathia—Cleveland Indians

In 2001, C. C. Sabathia won 17 games as a rookie with the Cleveland Indians. In 2007, he won the AL Cy Young Award with a 19–7 record. Only 26 years old, Sabathia had already won 100 games by the end of the 2007 season. In the middle of the 2008 season, he was traded to the Milwaukee Brewers of the National League Central division.

Joe Mauer and Justin Morneau—Minnesota Twins

In 2006, Twins catcher Joe Mauer became the first catcher to win the American League batting title, beating out Yankees shortstop Derek Jeter with a .347 average. Mauer made the American League All-Star team that year, fulfilling the promise the Twins saw in him when they made him the first overall selection in the 2001 amateur draft. Mauer's teammate, first baseman Justin Morneau, won the American League MVP award in 2006, hitting .321 with 34 homers and 130 RBI.

Kansas City Produces Winners

Though the Kansas City Royals have only had one winning season since 1994, the team has developed several players who went on to greater fame with other teams. This list includes All-Star Johnny Damon, who played on the Boston Red Sox team that won the 2004 World Series. In addition, the Royals system developed 1999 American League Rookie of the Year Carlos Beltrán, a star on the 2005 Houston Astros. The Royals continue to rebuild their team with talented young players, including third baseman Mark Teahen, outfielder Ross Gload, and designated hitter Billy Butler.

American League Central Award Winners
(since realignment in 1994)

American League MVP Award
1994: Frank Thomas (White Sox)
2006: Justin Morneau (Twins)

American League Rookie of the Year Award
1994: Bob Hamelin (Royals)
1995: Marty Cordova (Twins)
1999: Carlos Beltrán (Royals)
2003: Angel Berroa (Royals)
2006: Justin Verlander (Tigers)

American League Cy Young Award
1994: David Cone (Royals)
2004, 2006: Johan Santana (Twins)
2007: C. C. Sabathia (Indians)

Rolaids Relief Man of the Year Award
1995: José Mesa (Indians)
2000: Todd Jones (Indians)

World Series MVP Award
2005: Jermaine Dye (White Sox)

BASEBALL TRADITION IN THE AL CENTRAL

Of the five teams in the AL Central, four have existed since 1901. Three have spent those years located in the same city, developing their own traditions and building solid fan bases.

Minnesota Twins

The Washington Senators franchise relocated to Minnesota in 1961. The team had spent its first 60

Paws the Tiger *(left)* has been the official mascot of the Detroit Tigers since 1995. Paws entertains the crowd at Detroit's Comerica Park by meeting with fans and dancing.

The Metrodome is covered to protect players and fans from Minneapolis' cold weather. During play-off games, cheering fans fill the stadium, making it one of the loudest in baseball.

seasons in Washington, D.C., where it won one World Series championship, in 1924. The team settled in Minneapolis, Minnesota's largest city, and was renamed the Minnesota Twins, after the Twin Cities of Minneapolis and St. Paul. Fans and the local media sometimes refer to the team as the "Twinkies," a play on the team's name.

Beginning in 1982, the Twins played home games in the Hubert H. Humphrey Metrodome, an indoor stadium with artificial turf. However, the team's owners threatened for years to move to another city unless Minneapolis built a new stadium. The team will have a new ballpark in

2010, ending talk of relocation. The Twins are represented by a mascot named the TC Bear, a performer dressed in a bear costume complete with a Twins uniform shirt. The TC Bear often gets the home fans to wave their Homer Hankies—handkerchiefs printed with the Twins logo—to inspire the team during rallies. The Homer Hanky tradition started during the Twins' 1987 play-off run and remains strong to this day.

Cleveland Indians

In their history as a major league club, the Indians have been called the Cleveland Blues, the Cleveland Broncos, and the Cleveland Naps. They became the Indians in 1915, reportedly in honor of Native American player Louis Sockalexis. Fans often refer to the team as the "Wahoos" or "The Tribe." The Indians play at Progressive Field, formerly called Jacobs Field. "The Jake," as it is still called, was opened in 1994, replacing the old Municipal Stadium, which was demolished and turned into an artificial reef in Lake Erie.

The Indians' mascot and logo, a caricature of a Native American man that the organization calls Chief Wahoo, is one of the most controversial in professional sports. Many sports fans and Native American groups have called it racist and asked the team to change it, but ownership calls the logo a tradition—it's been around since the 1940s.

Indians fans believe strongly in curses. After trading away star slugger Rocky Colavito in 1960, the Indians failed to finish higher than third in the American League until the strike-shortened 1994 season. The Indians have since won two American League pennants but have not won a World Series since 1948. Some still blame the Curse of Rocky Colavito.

AMERICAN LEAGUE CENTRAL CITIES

Teams in the American League Central division all play in the Midwest. Chicago, Detroit, and Cleveland are all located in the Great Lakes region. Kansas City and Minneapolis, on the other hand, are located farther west.

Chicago White Sox

The Chicago White Sox were the Chicago White Stockings from 1901 to 1904, when the name was changed to the White Sox. Fan nicknames for the team have ranged from "The Go-Go White Sox" of the 1950s and the "Chicago Hit Men" of the 1980s to "The Good Guys" of today, a take on the team's current "Good Guys Wear Black" slogan.

The White Sox play at U.S. Cellular Field (formerly called Comiskey Park). The park was opened in 1991 to replace Old Comiskey Park, a landmark that had been built in 1910. The White Sox failed to win a

World Series championship from 1917 until 2005, a span of almost ninety years.

Kansas City Royals

The Royals franchise began playing in 1969, when the American League expanded. The team was brought into the city to replace the old Kansas City Athletics after that team's owner, Charles O. Finley, relocated to Oakland. The new owners decided to name their team for the Royal Livestock Show, an event that has been held in Kansas City since 1899.

The Royals play in Kauffman Stadium, named for team founder Ewing Kauffman. The stadium features elaborate fountains in the

Disco Demolition Night

On July 12, 1979, the Chicago White Sox invited local radio personality Steve Dahl to host an event called "Disco Demolition Night" at Comiskey Park. The promotion was conceived by Dahl after a rival station switched to an all-disco format. Dahl asked fans to bring in disco albums in exchange for a 98-cent admission price. The records would be collected in a crate and blown up on the field by Dahl between games of a doubleheader against the Tigers.

The promotion, however, went disastrously wrong. Organizers expected 5,000 fans to attend, but nearly 50,000 people showed up! Many fans were rowdy from the start, throwing records and even firecrackers onto the field. Dahl blew up the records on the field after the first game, as promised. Many fans took the destruction as a signal to begin rioting. They poured onto the field, destroying the batting cage, burning banners, and literally stealing the bases from the infield. Thirty-nine people were arrested for disorderly conduct, and the White Sox were forced to forfeit the second game.

outfield, a nod to Kansas City's reputation as the "City of Fountains."

Detroit Tigers

The Tigers were named after a military unit that was based in Detroit during the nineteenth century. Fans sometimes call them the "Bengals" or the "Tigs." They play in Comerica Park, opened in 2000 to replace venerable Tiger Stadium, which had been the team's home since 1912.

Royals owner Ewing Kauffman and his wife wave to the crowd during the 1985 World Series. With his great sense of civic pride, Kauffman was beloved in Kansas City.

In their long history, the Tigers have more AL pennants (10) than any other team in the AL Central. And they have won the World Series four times, more than any other team in the division. The chant "Eat 'em up, Tigers! Eat 'em up!" first became popular during Detroit's 1968 World Series run against the Cardinals. The chant was resurrected for 2006, when the team made the play-offs for the first time since 1987. Other rally cries include "Restore the roar" and the peculiar "It's gum time!" The latter slogan became popular during the 2006 season, after a camera in the dugout showed Tigers pitcher Nate Robertson stuffing gum into his mouth just before a late-inning Tigers rally.

GLOSSARY

charter member Member of a group present at the group's creation.

closer Relief pitcher brought in to protect a close lead for an inning or two at the end of a baseball game.

compile To put together.

Gold Glove Award Award given every year to the best defender at each position, as voted by the managers and coaches in each league.

lineup List of batters in the order in which they will bat.

no-hitter Game in which a pitcher or combination of pitchers does not give up a single hit.

payroll Total amount a business, company, or organization pays its employees.

play-offs Series of games designed to eliminate teams from contention before a championship series or game.

prolific Very productive.

resurrect To bring to view or use again.

rivalry In sports, an intense competition between teams or their fans.

rookie In baseball, a player who is in his first full year.

scout In baseball, a person whose job it is to assess the abilities of players.

venerable Worthy of respect.

FOR MORE INFORMATION

Major League Baseball
The Office of the Commissioner of Baseball
245 Park Avenue, 31st Floor
New York, NY 10167
(212) 931-7800
Web site: http://www.mlb.com
The commissioner's office oversees all aspects of Major League
Baseball.

National Baseball Hall of Fame and Museum
25 Main Street
Cooperstown, NY 13326
(888) HALL-OF-FAME (425-5633)
Web site: http://www.baseballhalloffame.org
The National Baseball Hall of Fame and Museum celebrates
and preserves the history of baseball.

Negro Leagues Baseball Museum
1616 East 18th Street
Kansas City, MO 64108
(816) 221-1920
Web site: http://www.nlbm.com
The Negro Leagues Baseball Museum honors great African
American baseball players who were once excluded from
Major League Baseball.

(Note: Links to official team Web sites are available at the Rosenlinks URL, listed below.)

Web Sites

Due to the changing nature of Internet links, Rosen Publishing has developed an online list of Web sites related to the subject of this book. This site is updated regularly. Please use this link to access the list:

http://www.rosenlinks.com/imlb/amlc

FOR FURTHER READING

Altergott, Hannah. *Great Teams in Baseball History*. Milwaukee, WI: Raintree Publishing, 2006.

Asinof, Eliot. *Eight Men Out: The Black Sox and the 1919 World Series*. New York, NY: Henry Holt and Company, 1987.

Fischer, David. *Baseball Top 10*. New York, NY: DK Publishing, Inc., 2004.

Forker, Dom, et al. *Baffling Baseball Trivia*. Madison, WI: Main Street Press, 2004.

Formosa, Dan, and Paul Hamburger. *Baseball Field Guide: An In-Depth Illustrated Guide to the Complete Rules of Baseball*. New York, NY: Thunder's Mouth Press, 2006.

Goldman, Steven, ed. *Baseball Prospectus 2008: The Essential Guide to the 2008 Baseball Season*. New York, NY: Perseus Books Group, 2008.

Light, Jonathan Fraser. *The Cultural Encyclopedia of Baseball*. Jefferson, NC: McFarland & Company, Inc., 2005.

Lipsyte, Robert. *Heroes of Baseball: The Men Who Made It America's Favorite Game*. New York, NY: Atheneum Books for Young Readers, 2006.

Thorn, John, ed., et al. *Total Baseball, Completely Revised and Updated: The Ultimate Baseball Encyclopedia*. Wilmington, DE: SportClassic Books, 2004.

Wong, Stephen. *Baseball Treasures*. New York, NY: HarperCollins, 2007.

BIBLIOGRAPHY

Alvarez, Mark, ed. *The Perfect Game*. Dallas, TX: The Taylor Publishing Company, 2003.

Beaton, Rod. "No Anniversary Party for Disco Debacle." *USA Today*, July 12, 2004. Retrieved March 15, 2008 (http://www.usatoday.com/sports/baseball/2004-07-12-disco-demolition-anniversary_x.htm).

Bryson, Michael G. *The Twenty-Four-Inch Home Run and Other Outlandish, Incredible But True Events in Baseball History*. Chicago, IL: Contemporary Books, 1990.

Foreman, Sean. Sports Reference, LLC, 2000–2008. Baseball-Reference.com. Retrieved March 15, 2008 (http://www.baseball-reference.com).

Goldman, Steven, ed. *It Ain't Over 'Til It's Over: The Baseball Prospectus Pennant Race Book*. New York, NY: Perseus Book Group, 2007.

Justice, Richard. "Sparky Anderson Elected to Hall of Fame; Only Manager to Win World Series in Both Leagues; Negro Leagues' Stearnes In." *Washington Post*, March 1, 2000. Retrieved March 15, 2008 (http://www.highbeam.com/doc/1P2-512019.html).

Koppett, Leonard. *Koppett's Concise History of Major League Baseball*. New York, NY: Carroll & Graf Publishers, 2004.

Kuenster, John. *Heartbreakers: Baseball's Most Agonizing Defeats*. Chicago, IL: Ivan R. Dee Publisher, 2001.

Levenson, Barry. *The Seventh Game: The 35 World Series That Have Gone the Distance*. New York, NY: McGraw-Hill, 2004.

Lowe, John. "Curtis Granderson Cuts His Offseason Short, Eager to Get Back to Work." *Detroit Free Press*, February 14, 2008. Retrieved March 15, 2008 (http://www.freep.com/apps/pbcs.dll/article?AID=/20080214/SPORTS02/802140436/1050).

Merkin, Scott. "How Sweep It Is for the White Sox!" MLB.com, October 27, 2005. Retrieved March 15, 2008 (http://mlb.mlb.com/news/gameday_recap.jsp?ymd=20051026&content_id=1260213&vkey=recap&fext=.jsp&c_id=cws).

O'Connell, Kevin, and Josh Pahigian. *The Ultimate Baseball Road-Trip: A Fan's Guide to Major League Stadiums*. Guilford, CT: The Lyons Press, 2004.

Ohio EPA's Public Interest Center. "News Release: City of Cleveland Allowed to Create Reefs in Lake Erie." August 20, 1997. Retrieved March 15, 2008 (http://www.epa.state.oh.us/pic/nr/1997/august/stad401.html).

Seymour, Harold. *Baseball: The People's Game*. New York, NY: Oxford University Press, 1990.

Singer, Tom. "Shared Stories Weave Through ALCS." MLB.com, October 9, 2007. Retrieved March 15, 2008 (http://mlb.mlb.com/news/article.jsp?ymd=20071008&content_id=2257555&vkey=ps2007news&fext=.jsp&c_id=mlb).

Sporting News. "Gum Time!" June 1, 2006. Retrieved March 15, 2008 (http://www.sportingnews.com/blog/L_Pennants/19945).

INDEX

About the Author

Jason Porterfield is a writer living in Chicago. He has authored more than twenty books for Rosen Publishing, covering topics from American history to college basketball. His sports titles for Rosen include *Baseball: Rules, Tips, Strategy, and Safety*; *Kurt Busch: NASCAR Driver*; *Basketball in the ACC (Atlantic Coast Conference)*; and *Basketball in the Big East Conference*.

Photo Credits

Cover, p. 1 (all photos), pp. 4–5 (both photos), 7 (background), 10, 14 (background), 17, 21 (background), 23, 25, 27, 28 (both photos), 30, 31, 32, 35 (both photos), 36 © Getty Images; p. 7 (foreground), pp. 8, 13, 14 (foreground), 20, 21 (foreground) AP Photos; p. 15 © AFP/Getty Photos; p. 40 © Focus on Sport/Getty Images.

Designer: Sam Zavieh; Editor: Christopher Roberts
Photo Researcher: Marty Levick